KT-157-058

TREASURE ISLAND

BASED ON THE BOOK BY
ROBERT LOUIS STEVENSON

TREASURE ISLAND

BASED ON THE BOOK BY
ROBERT LOUIS STEVENSON

Retold by Henry Brook

Reading consultant: Alison Kelly

Edited by Jane Chisholm and Rachel Firth

Designed by Matthew Preston

Cover illustration by Ryan Quickfall

Inside illustrations by Ian McNee

First published in 2018 by Usborne Publishing Ltd., Usborne House,
83-85 Saffron Hill, London EC1N 8RT, England.
www.usborne.com

Copyright © Usborne Publishing 2018

Illustrations copyright © Usborne Publishing 2018

The name Usborne and the devices 🎈🌐 are Trade Marks of
Usborne Publishing Ltd. UE

All rights reserved. No part of this publication may be reproduced, stored in a retrieval
system or transmitted in any form or by any means, electronic, mechanical,
photocopying, recording or otherwise without the prior permission of the publisher.

A CIP catalogue record for this book is available from the British Library.

CONTENTS

CHAPTER ONE

THE TIDE BRINGS A STRANGER

I remember the stranger as if it were yesterday. When I first spotted him he was plodding up the cliff path towards the Admiral Benbow inn where I lived with my father and mother. As he came closer I could see that he was a sea dog, sun-scorched and tall, with a greasy pigtail sprouting from under his peaked hat. A servant followed after him, dragging an enormous sea chest. But the stranger acted as though he was alone in the deserted bay where our inn stood, whistling and humming to himself. As he turned his head, I saw the white scar of a sword wound across his cheek. Suddenly, he burst into song, in a voice broken by years of storms and struggles at sea:

"Fifteen men on the dead man's chest,
Yo-ho-ho and a bottle of rum…"

The stranger rapped on our front door and bellowed: "Landlord, bring me rum." My father hurried out with a bottle and a glass.

"I like this cove," said the seaman, sipping his drink. "Do you get much company?"

"Very little," replied my father, "more's the pity."

"But that's just how I like it," laughed the seaman. "This is the place for me. All I need is rum, a bed, bacon and eggs, and that cliff up there to keep a lookout for ships. You can call me captain."

He scattered a handful of gold coins around my father's feet.

"Tell me when you want more. Now bring that chest," he shouted over his shoulder to the servant. Snatching the rum bottle from my startled father, he marched inside.

Even with his shabby clothes and coarse speech, the seaman had the habits of a commander used to giving orders. His servant was soon sent running for home, glad to be free of such a gruff master.

By day, our captain kept to himself, prowling the cliffs and peering out to sea through a brass telescope. When night came, he would sit in a corner, drinking rum and glowering at anyone who ventured too close.

He was always asking me about any strangers calling at the inn. When a sailor did stop in for a drink, our captain would peep around the door to watch him and keep silent until the man had left. A few days after his arrival, the captain took me into his confidence. "Come here, boy," he hissed. "Do a job for me and you can earn a silver coin on the first of each month."

"Of course, sir," I answered.

"I want you to keep your weather-eye open for a seafaring man," he whispered. "A man with one leg. If you spy him, come running to me."

I watched the cliffs and lonely moors behind the inn for this man with one leg. He was so much in my thoughts he began to haunt my dreams. On stormy nights, when the wind shook the shutters and the breaking surf boomed around the cove, I saw him in a thousand hideous shapes.

My fear of the one-legged man made me less afraid of the captain, but he terrified our other guests. On nights when the rum had been flowing, he would sing wicked sea songs and tell blood-chilling stories of shipwrecks and typhoons. He ordered everyone in the bar to accompany him in a chorus of his *Yo-ho-ho, and a bottle of rum*, and our regular customers would join in for dear life, afraid of annoying the seadog. Only when he staggered off to his room was his audience permitted to leave.

The captain's stories frightened people. He described hangings and men being made to walk the plank, pirate raids and massacres, all in the most gruesome detail. If only a tiny part of what he said was true, he must have lived among the worst killers ever to set sail on the ocean. The language was so wild, some of the simple country folk covered their ears in shame.

My father feared our customers would be driven away. Secretly, I thought the local people liked to be scared, as their lives were so dull. But whether he repelled or attracted listeners, the captain was certainly ruining us. His stay stretched on, month after month, but my father was too timid to ask him for more of his gold. When he dared to raise the subject of the bill, the captain snorted so loudly it sounded like a lion's roar and then fixed him with an ugly stare. It was a terrible burden on my father's nerves and his health began to suffer.

It was after one of Dr. Livesey's visits to my poor father's bedside that I finally saw the captain meet his match. The doctor was in the bar smoking his pipe and chatting with a local man while waiting for a groom to bring his horse. I had noticed the striking difference between the smart doctor, with his powdered wig as white as snow, and the plain country folk we served at the inn. However, the greatest contrast was with that filthy scarecrow of a pirate lounging in a corner, bleary-eyed with rum.

Suddenly, the captain broke into his song:

"Fifteen men on the dead man's chest,
Yo-ho-ho, and a bottle of rum!
Drink and the devil had done for the rest,
Yo-ho-ho, and a bottle of rum!"

I was so used to the tune by now, I ignored it, but I noticed Dr. Livesey glance up angrily from his conversation. A moment later, the captain slammed his fist on the table, hard enough to leave a mark. This was his signal for silence. Every voice in the inn stopped at once, all except for Dr. Livesey, who carried on talking.

The captain glared across the room but when this had no effect he beat the table again. "Quiet there," he barked. "No talking between decks."

"Were you addressing me, sir?" asked the doctor.

With an oath, the captain made it clear that he was.

"In that case," the doctor replied, calmly, "I have only one thing to say to you. Keep drinking and the world will soon be rid of a very dirty scoundrel."

The old seadog jumped up and snatched a sailor's knife from his pocket. "I'll pin you to the wall!" he shouted.

"Put that away," replied the doctor steadily, "or I promise as a gentleman that you shall hang for it."

Both men glowered at one another, but it was the captain who backed down. He sheathed his knife and sat down like a whipped dog.

"I'm a magistrate, you know," the doctor added. "If I hear a word of a complaint against you, I'll have you hunted down."

In a moment, the groom arrived with the doctor's horse and Livesey rode away. The captain was quiet for the rest of that night, and for many nights to come.

CHAPTER TWO

KILLER IN THE FOG

Not long after the doctor's visit we had the first of the mysterious visitors who would finally free us of our captain, while dragging us deeper into his secret business. It had been a hard winter, with gales lashing the coast. Nobody expected my poor, sick father to survive into the spring. He was confined to bed, leaving my mother and me too busy running the inn to pay much attention to our unwelcome guest.

Early one January morning, when the frost was glistening around the cove, I heard the captain shuffle from his room. I stepped over to my window to see what he was up to and saw him making for the beach, his cutlass blade swinging under the folds of his old blue coat and the brass telescope glinting under his arm. It was so cold, his breath hung in the air like smoke and I thought I could hear him snorting with rage, as though he was still thinking of the good doctor.

My mother was upstairs and I was laying the table for breakfast when I heard the front door creak and a man entered. He was a pale, twitching, sickly creature, with two fingers missing from his left hand. There was a sword at his side, but he didn't look like a fighting man. I still had my monthly coin from the captain for reports of any seafarers, so I studied the man carefully. He didn't look like a sailor, but there was something about him that reminded me of the restless sea.

"Bring rum," said the man. He pointed at the table where I was laying out the breakfast things. "Is this for my mate, Billy Bones?" he asked, slyly.

"I don't know your friend," I replied. "It's for a guest we call Captain."

"That's about right," said the man, stroking his bony chin. "That's the kind of name my mate Bill would give himself. He's got a scar on his cheek and a gentle way about him when he's got rum in his belly." The man smiled as he saw my reaction. "Is he up in his room?" he asked.

"He's out on one of his walks."

"I think I'll wait for him," chuckled the man. "He'll be right pleased to see me."

I didn't like the expression on his face, but I decided it wasn't any of my business, so I went back to my chores.

"Well, here he is," called the man, peering out through the window. "You and me will just step behind the door and give him a nice surprise."

He pushed me into a gloomy corner behind the open door and I saw that he was gripping the hilt of his cutlass and the muscles in his face were twitching in fright. The captain entered and walked over to his breakfast table.

"Bill!" called the stranger, stepping into the light.

The captain spun on his heel and I was shocked by the look on his face – as though he was staring at a ghost, or the devil.

"Come, Bill," cooed the man. "Don't you remember an old shipmate?"

"Black Dog," the captain gasped. "What do you want?"

"You were never a man for small talk," laughed Black Dog. "Let's have a glass of rum and a talk."

I left the two men at their table with a bottle. After a few minutes their voices grew louder and I heard the captain booming: "Never! You can go to the scaffold for all I care."

There was an explosion of swearing and the sound of furniture being toppled. I heard the ring of steel on steel and a yelp of pain. When I rushed to look into the room, I saw Black Dog dashing into the road, blood oozing from his shoulder. The captain chased after him, lifting his sword.

He would have sliced Black Dog from crown to chin if his sword hadn't caught the wooden Admiral Benbow sign that hangs over our door. You can still see the notch he cut into the side of it.

Black Dog scampered away and the captain came staggering back into the inn. "Bring me rum, Jim," he called. "Rum, and then I must leave."

I darted to the bar and heard a mighty crash behind me. The captain had collapsed to the floor and lay among the broken glass and splinters of wood left behind from the fight. My mother had heard the noise and hurried downstairs to join me at his side.

"Oh, Jim," she cried. "What a disgrace on our house, these pirates fighting."

The captain's face was a bloodless white and his breathing came loud and hard.

"Let's get some rum into him," my mother suggested, but his teeth were locked together as tight as a vice. Dr. Livesey then appeared at the door, on his way to call on my father.

"Doctor," I called, "where is he wounded? I can't see any wound."

"He's no more wounded than you or I," scoffed the doctor. "He's had a stroke from his drinking, just as I warned. Mrs. Hawkins, you go up to see that your husband is well, while I try to save this ruffian's worthless life. Jim, fetch a basin."

When I returned, the doctor had rolled up the captain's sleeve, exposing a great sinewy arm covered in tattoos. Billy Bones was marked in black ink next to a faded sketch of a gallows and a man hanging from its rope.

"Let's have a pint out of you, Mr. Bones," laughed the doctor. "You're not afraid of blood, are you, Jim?"

"No, sir," I answered firmly.

The doctor took a lot of blood before the captain opened his eyes. He frowned at the doctor, but looked relieved when he saw me. "Where's Black Dog?" he gasped.

"There's no black dog here," replied the doctor.

"You've been drinking rum and you've had a stroke, and if you don't stop drinking, you'll die. I'd stake my wig on it. Now let's get him to bed, Jim. He needs a few days of rest."

I let the captain sleep until noon and then took him a cool glass of water. He was sitting up in his bed and his eyes looked weak but excited.

"You're the only one I can trust, Jim," he cried. "Now fetch me a jug of rum."

"But the doctor's orders?" I protested.

"Doctors are all swabs," he spat. "I've been through earthquakes and yellow fever, and it was rum that kept me alive. With no rum I get the horrors. I've just seen old Flint smiling at me from the corner, plain as day. Just get me one glass."

I was worried that the noise he was making might disturb my father, who was weaker than ever, so I brought him a cup of rum and watched him drain it in one greedy gulp.

"That's better," he hissed. "Now I've got to get moving. They're already circling like hungry sharks

– they'll lay the Black Spot on me if I stay. They've spent what they had and want to steal mine, but I'll leave them lost in a maze of reefs and slip away."

He tried to swing his legs off the bed, but he was too weak to stand, and he sank back, groaning onto the sheets.

"They want my chest," he growled. "You must ride to the doctor and bring the soldiers. Bring them and they'll catch Flint's crew. I was his first mate, Jim. He gave me the chest at Savannah, when he lay dying of fever. But don't raise the alarm until they come with the Black Spot, or if you see the man with one leg. He's the worst of them all, Jim."

"But what is the Black Spot?" I asked him.

"Justice," he replied, in a hushed voice. "Keep your eyes open, and I'll give you a share of everything."

As he spoke, his eyes closed and he fell into a deep sleep, leaving me more confused than ever.

I had little time to worry about spots and old

Flint, whoever he was, for that same evening my father died. The captain drank more than ever, while I worked without sleep to keep the inn open and comfort my poor mother.

The day after my father's funeral, I was gazing out towards the cove when I noticed a lone figure approaching. He tapped at the path with a long stick and wore a green cloth shade fixed over his eyes and nose, and I guessed he must be blind. Hunched over with age, he wore a tattered old sea cloak with a hood that made him appear twisted and deformed. I had never seen a shabbier, more dreadful-looking creature.

"Is there a kind lad here," he called out, "who will help a man who lost his eyes fighting for king and country? Will you guide me to the inn?"

I reached out to help him and his long fingers closed around my wrist like steel claws.

"Take me to the captain," he snarled, "or I'll snap your arm in two."

I had never heard a voice so cruel, cold and ugly.

He gripped my arm as I took him inside. The captain was slumped over one of the tables in the bar, but when he raised his eyes he looked like a man staring death in the face.

"Boy," snapped the blind man, "give me his left hand. Don't you move, Bill."

I slowly lifted the captain's huge, open palm and the blind man slipped something between his fingers.

"It's done," he hissed. He released my arm, retraced his steps across the room and went tap-tap-tapping out into the fog.

CHAPTER THREE

THE BLACK SPOT

Like a man coming slowly out of a trance, it took the captain several seconds to stare down at his open hand.

"Ten o'clock," he cried. "That's only six hours, but we'll beat them yet."

He staggered to his feet, but the sudden effort was too much for his heart. I watched him lift a shaking hand to his throat and then crash face-first onto the floorboards.

There was no use hurrying for the doctor. The captain was dead. Even though I had lived in fear of the man, I had also pitied him for his drinking. My cheeks were wet with tears when my mother arrived. I quickly told her everything I knew, including the strange tale of old Flint.

"We're in danger if they come back, Jim," said my mother. "We must go to the village and ask for help to defend the inn."

As soon as darkness fell, we hurried through the ice-cold fog, listening for any strange sounds in the night air. My heart soared when I saw the village lanterns in the next cove, but not a soul would agree to join us at the inn. As soon as I mentioned the name Flint, the men shrank away in terror. Other villagers said they'd seen strangers on the cliff paths and a ship with no flag at anchor in the bay. They wanted nothing to do with pirates and would only agree to ride for Livesey and raise the alarm.

"The inn is all I have left for my boy," cried my mother. "If that dead pirate has any gold, some of it belongs to us. We'll open his chest, Jim, even if we have to go alone."

My heart was beating wildly as we slipped back around the cove, and I let out a sigh of relief when the heavy oak door of the Admiral Benbow was bolted behind us. My mother lit a candle and we stepped over to the captain's body. His eyes were open and glaring, and one arm was stretched out in a last spasm of pain.

"Close the window shutters, Jim," said my mother, "and then help me find the key to his chest," she added, with a shudder. "It must be somewhere about his corpse."

I knelt by the captain at once, sparing my mother this terrible task. Next to his outstretched hand I noticed a torn circle of paper, dark with ink on one side – the Black Spot. I turned it over and saw the scrawled words:

You have until ten tonight.

"They'll be here at ten bells," I gasped. As the words left my lips, our old clock began striking, but luck was with us.

"That's only six," said my mother. "Get the key."

I rummaged in his pockets and pulled out a pile of sailor's junk: a needle and thread, coins, tobacco, his knife and a compass.

"Try his neck," hissed my mother.

I padded my fingers around the cold flesh under his shirt and found a loop of greasy string. Using the captain's own knife, I cut the key free.

We hurried to his room and dragged the old chest from under his bed. The initial 'B' was branded into the wood, and the corners were all chipped and worn. My mother quickly tried the key and the lid swung open to release a pungent smell of tar and tobacco.

Under a fine suit of clothes we found the essentials of the captain's life: a small quadrant for taking map readings, a bar of solid silver, four pistols with intricate carving on the grips, a Spanish watch and a clutch of exotic shells lifted from tropical sands. Lying beneath the shells was an old sea cloak, crusted white with salt from a thousand ocean voyages.

We lifted the cloak and found a parcel of papers and a sack of coins.

"I only want what we're owed," said my mother, proudly. "Not a penny more."

The coins were so various they seemed to have been collected from every port and country around the world. As I fumbled to pick out a gold guinea, I heard a noise that made my blood flash cold – the tap of a stick on the frozen path. My mother stared at me, wide-eyed, as we heard a knock at the outside door and the bolt rattled. After a few terrified seconds of silence, I heard the sound of tapping again, fading as the blind man walked away into the fog.

"No time for counting, mother," I whispered. "Hurry, take it all."

"But I'm an honest woman," she protested. "I've almost enough."

We heard a whistle from the hill above the inn.

"This will do," cried my mother, grabbing a handful of the coins.

"And I'll take this," I said, snatching up the bundle of papers, "to make up the difference."

We left the candle burning in the dead captain's room and groped our way downstairs. I quickly unbolted the door, and we stepped into the night. The fog was clearing now, but the door and the bar windows of the inn were still covered. It was just thick enough to save us, for I heard footsteps and could see a lantern dancing towards us through the curls of white.

"Take the money and run, Jim," my mother shouted.

I cursed my mother's honesty for keeping us counting the coins so long, but as the fog swirled to one side, I saw a chance to escape. There was a stone bridge crossing the road before our inn. I grabbed my mother's wrist and dragged her under the arch of the bridge. The fog over the stream was just thick enough to hide us from searchers around the inn. I peeped over the bank of the stream and saw seven men burst out of the white wall of fog.

"Kick down the door," screeched a voice that made me tremble. It was the blind man, at the back of the group, holding the hand of the last man.

"Aye, aye, sir," called two men. They burst inside and I could hear the sounds of stamping feet and crashing doors.

"Bill's dead," came a shout.

"Search him," snapped the blind man, "find the key."

I heard the raiders ransacking the captain's room and then a window flew open and I saw a man's head in the moonlight.

"Pew," he called, "they've been here before us. The chest's open."

"Is it there?" screamed the blind man.

"Most of the money is."

"Curse the money. Are Flint's papers there?"

"Gone," shouted the man in the window.

The moon was so bright I could see Pew's lips curl back over his teeth in rage.

"It's the boy," he howled. "I wish I'd blinded him.

Scatter lads, he can't be far. Seek him out."

The house exploded with noise as the gang searched for us. They rushed outside and soon began prodding at the bushes along the road. I was sure they would find us, but as they came closer I heard two whistles from the hill.

"That's the alarm," shrieked one man. "Let's be away."

"You're not running yet!" screamed Pew. "Find that woman and the boy."

The group of men didn't run, but they glanced at each other nervously.

"You're close to millions," spat Pew. "Why should I be a beggar for the rest of my days when I could be rich as a lord? Catch them."

"We've got the coins," pleaded one of the men.

Pew's rage welled up in him and he began striking at his gang with his stick. I heard horses and a pistol shot from the cove. The men broke away, running in all directions, leaving Pew behind.

"Morgan, Black Dog," called Pew, desperately.

"Don't leave old Pew, mates."

Four riders clattered out of the fog at the top of the hill, charging down the road. Pew screamed in terror and turned to run. He stumbled and tottered and in his panic he tripped into the path of the first horse.

The rider tried to stop but it was too late. Pew let out an awful scream and I saw him trampled and crushed. It was the end of the blind man.

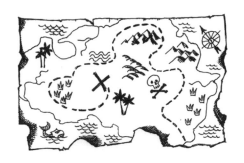

CHAPTER FOUR

FLINT'S SECRET

I ran over to meet the riders and recognized one of them as Captain Dance, leader of a customs patrol. He listened as I told him everything, then dismounted to join my mother as she went to inspect the inn. Every stick of furniture was smashed and I saw at once that we were ruined.

"What on earth were they searching for?" cried Captain Dance.

"I believe I have the answer in my jacket pocket, sir," I replied. "And I think it would be a good idea to show it to Dr. Livesey."

"He's a wise gentleman," agreed Captain Dance. "He's up at Squire Trelawney's house tonight, I believe. This man on the road is dead, and though he looks a scoundrel I must make an official report to the squire. We can ride to his house together."

I said a quick goodbye to my mother and then jumped up behind one of the riders. In an instant, we set off at a fast trot along the coast road. We soon entered a long, moonlit avenue that led to the squire's grand house. A butler led us in silence into a great library. The squire and the doctor were seated by a fire, puffing at their pipes.

I was only a country boy, and had never been this close to the squire before. He was tall and thickset, with a face that was lined and tanned from years of travel. His great, bushy eyebrows made him look as fierce as a bird of prey.

"Hello, Jim," called the doctor, "what good wind blows you in here?"

The captain made his report of the events at the inn and the death of Pew. The squire cried "Bravo!"

and the two men jumped up from their seats when they heard how my mother had been brave enough to return to the inn.

"Fine work, Dance," said the squire, pacing about the room. "And as for that rascal, Pew, you have done us all a service getting rid of him. This boy Hawkins is clearly a good lad."

"He's earned a piece of pie," smiled the doctor.

"Indeed he has," boomed the squire. "Dance, go down to the kitchen and ask for some ale for yourself and some pie for the boy. Then you must be off on the King's business with your patrol."

"Thank you, sir," replied Dance and he stepped out of the room.

A few minutes later, I was tucking into a large wedge of pigeon pie. The squire and the doctor were back in their seats by the fire.

"You've heard of this Flint before?" asked the doctor.

"Heard of him?" roared the squire. "He was the most bloodthirsty buccaneer to lift a sword. I've seen his ship with my own eyes, sir, off Trinidad. My captain was such a coward, he ran for port when he saw the pirate's sails on the horizon."

"Did he have much money?" asked the doctor, calmly.

"Money?" bellowed the squire. "He had a treasure of coins and jewels beyond counting. If we have a clue to where it is, I shall take you and Hawkins to Bristol, fit out a ship and we'll find the gold if it takes a year of searching."

"In that case," chuckled the doctor, "let's ask Jim's permission to open the papers he's brought us."

The doctor carefully unfolded the bundle, releasing a small book from a roll of parchment.

"Look at the markings in this book," cried the squire.

Numbers and dates were arranged in rows across each page. I peered closer and saw one line that said: June 12, 1745 – 70 pounds taken – off Caracas, Venezuela.

"What can it mean?" asked the doctor.

"It's clear as day, man," the squire replied. "This is the rogue's account book, giving the date, the location and the prize from each pirate attack. God help those poor souls off Caracas, thrown to the sharks no doubt. And look at the dates on the last page, almost twenty years later than the first page."

"Billy Bones was prowling the oceans, collecting a fortune," said the doctor.

"Let's see the other item," the squire demanded.

The doctor spread the parchment over the table and we saw the sketch of an island, with the names of hills and other details. The land was nine miles long and five wide, shaped like a fat little dragon standing on its heels. There were three, blood-red crosses scratched into the map, and one had some writing below it:

Tall tree atop hill. Go ten feet southeast. Arms and silver are easily found in the sandhill.

J.F.

"Livesey, we've got it!" roared the squire. "I'll go to Bristol tomorrow to make arrangements. Join me in ten days and we'll have the best ship and crew in England. Hawkins shall be cabin boy and you can be ship's doctor. We'll take my best three servants and reach the island in no time. Then we'll have money to wallow in for the rest of our days."

"Squire Trelawney," interrupted the doctor, looking serious, "I will join you and work my heart out to find this treasure, but there is one man involved in this business who makes me nervous."

"Name the dog!" boomed the squire.

"You," snapped the doctor. "You're a chatterbox, sir, and there are men out there who would cut our throats for this map. You must promise not to breathe a word to another soul."

"You may count on me," answered the squire. "I'll be as silent as the grave."

CHAPTER FIVE

THE SEA COOK

With my mother's permission, I lived at the hall for several weeks, helping the squire's servants to prepare for our voyage and dreaming of the sea. The map of Treasure Island was fixed in my mind. I brooded over the parchment sketch for hours, exploring every hill and valley in my imagination. But, in all my daydreams of wild beasts, cannibals and rocky shores, there was nothing as strange as what really happened.

At last, we received a letter from the squire, addressed to everyone leaving on the voyage.

Livesey was away in London, searching for a doctor who might be willing to look after his patients for a few months. The head servant, Redruth, had been a poor student at school, so I read it aloud for him:

Old Anchor Inn, Bristol

Dear Friends,

The ship is ready and hungry for the sea. You've never seen a sweeter schooner – the Hispaniola.

I have made many friends here – all keen to help the moment they heard about our quest to find treasure.

"Oh, no," I cried, "the squire's been chatting. The doctor won't be happy."

"The squire can say what he wants," snapped Redruth, loyally. "Read on."

Some say I bought the Hispaniola *for twice what it's worth, but I call them fools. I can tell a jewel of a ship when I see one.*

We've had trouble hiring a crew. We need 20 brave men, but I could only find a handful, until I had a piece of good luck. I was strolling along the docks when I met an old sailor. He keeps an inn in the town with his Caribbean wife and knows all the best seafaring men along the coast. Life on dry land was making him unwell, he told me, and he was desperate to get to sea again as a ship's cook. He'd hobbled to the docks that day just to get a sniff of the sea air.

Long John Silver is his name. He served under our navy's Captain Hawke, and lost his leg in battle for our King. I offered him a job at once.

Silver soon introduced me to some of the toughest salts you could imagine, not pretty, but good fighting men for a crew. He even helped me to weed out a few weaklings from the sailors I'd already taken on. They lacked stamina and experience, he told me.

I am as fit as a fiddle, eat like a bull, sleep like a log but I'm longing to taste saltwater spray on my lips again. Forget the treasure, the ocean is the greater glory. Make full speed to Bristol!

Yours, John Trelawney

When I'd read this letter I was trembling with excitement, unlike old Redruth, who only complained about his miserable luck. He never wanted to leave his village, let alone England.

We left for the Admiral Benbow the following morning and I was relieved to find my mother in good health. Squire Trelawney had paid to repair all the damages at the inn, and even hired a young lad to take my place, helping in the bar.

I cried that night at the thought of everything I was leaving behind. The next afternoon, I said goodbye to my mother and the cove where I had always lived and set off briskly along the cliff path. A mail coach met us at the next village, and we rode through the night to reach Bristol.

The squire's inn was close to the docks. As we walked across to it, I saw great fleets of ships at anchor. The sailors on one ship were singing on the decks, on the next they were high in the rigging, hanging to ropes that looked no thicker than spiderwebs. At every step, I saw something extraordinary. Huge figureheads towered up from the prow of each ship, faded from years of roaming the oceans. Old sailors pushed past me on every side. They had rings in their ears, and sported long pigtails and curly beards.

While I was still dazzled by everything I had seen, we met squire Trelawney coming out of his inn. He wore a sea officer's uniform and a broad smile on his face.

"Here they are," he said, "and the doctor joined me last night so the ship's company is complete. We sail tomorrow."

After treating me to breakfast at the inn, the squire sent me off with a message for his new friend, Silver.

"His tavern is called the Spyglass," he told me. "Look out for a telescope over the door."

I set off along another quay, busy with sailors, merchants and their carts. The tavern was nearby, but the drinkers inside looked a rough lot. I hung by the door for a moment, almost afraid to enter.

While I waited, I saw a man step out from behind the bar. His left leg was cut off close to the hip and he used a crutch under his left shoulder. He was very strong and nimble, hopping about like a bird. His face was huge, and he looked friendly and intelligent, whistling and chatting with his customers as he swung between the tables.

From the first mention of Long John, I had feared that he might be the same monster that Captain Billy Bones had hired me to look out for. However, one glance at the neat man banished all my doubts. I stepped into the room and introduced myself to the landlord.

"Oh, you're here on the squire's business," he laughed loudly. "You must be our cabin boy, Jim Hawkins."

He shook my hand in his giant fist and I stared into his pale eyes. But I still noticed a movement at the side of the room. A man had jumped up and run outside. I only caught a glimpse of him but it was enough to see it was that rogue, Black Dog.

"Stop him!" I cried. "He's a pirate."

"And he didn't pay his bill," roared Silver. "Catch

him, lads." One of the drinkers nodded and sprinted into the street. "You, Morgan," said Silver, calling to another man. "You were drinking with him. Did you know he was a pirate, this Black Dog?"

"No, sir," said the man, meekly. "I'd only just met him."

"That's lucky for you," Silver replied fiercely. "I can't have criminals like that wandering into my inn. It strikes me I've seen him before. He came in with a blind beggar."

"Pew," I shouted.

"He looked a real shark," Silver gasped. "I hope we catch this Dog fellow and we can present him to the squire."

"Silver," came a voice. It was the runner that had gone after Black Dog. "I lost him in a crowd by the dock."

"Oh, that's a shame," said Silver, looking downcast. "In the old days, before I had a stump of oak for a leg, I would have caught him myself in a flash. Let's weigh anchor and find the squire so we can report what's happened, but try to spare a soft word for me, lad. This is a stain on my character."

Silver led me along the quay, pointing out ships and describing them as though he'd sailed in every one of them. He even taught me some words that sailors use and I began to see that he was the best possible shipmate.

We found the squire taking a drink with the doctor and Silver quickly told them everything.

"A shame we couldn't nab him," said the squire, "but it can't be helped. Make sure you're on deck by four this afternoon, Silver."

"Aye, aye, sir," answered the cook.

"Well, Trelawney," said the doctor, when Silver had disappeared into the crowd on the quay, "I don't know about your other work here, but I like this John Silver."

"He's solid as a rock," declared the squire. "And now, doctor, it's time Jim saw the ship."

CHAPTER SIX

CAPTAIN SMOLLETT

Our schooner was anchored off the docks, and we had to row out to her. We pulled alongside her dripping boards and were saluted by a tanned old sailor, Mr. Arrow. He helped us clamber aboard, and it was clear from their chatter that he and the squire were already firm friends. The same was not true with the captain, Mr. Smollett, a sharp-faced, frosty-looking man, who seemed angry with everything on board. He gave the squire a stern glance and requested an urgent meeting in the main cabin.

"Well, captain," the squire began, "I hope everything's shipshape and to your liking."

"It's not, sir," snapped the captain, checking that the cabin door was shut tight. "I believe it's best to speak plainly, even if it offends. I don't like this voyage of yours, the crew, or the mate, Mr. Arrow."

"I suppose you don't like my ship either?" roared the squire, in anger.

"She looks a fine vessel, sir."

"And what about me, sir," the squire continued. "Do you care for me?"

"Let's be calm, squire," said the doctor, in a soothing voice. "I think the captain has said too much or too little and I want to know which it is. Explain why you don't like our voyage, captain."

"The squire didn't think to tell me," replied the captain, crossing his arms, "but I have learned from the crew that this is a treasure hunt. And hunting treasure is dangerous. I don't like it, least of all when everyone onboard seems to be in on the secret – including the cook's parrot – except for me. Your secret is out in the open, gentlemen, and you'll be lucky to escape with your lives."

"That's very clear," said Livesey. "But we've accepted the risks involved. Next, tell me why you don't like the crew."

"The mate's been drinking rum with the men," answered Smollett. "They won't respect him if he's too friendly."

"Are you saying he's a drunkard?" asked the squire.

"I'm only saying he needs to keep away from the men," replied Smollett.

"What do you want us to do?" asked the doctor.

"Are you determined to go on this voyage?" the captain answered.

"We're set like iron," said the squire.

"Then listen to my suggestions. Move all the arms and gunpowder to the strong room under this room. Our cabins are nearby and we can keep control of the weapons here. Have your own men sleep at this end of the ship, away from the sailors who berth near the prow. And there's one more thing. There's been too much blabbing…"

"Indeed there has," nodded the doctor.

"I've heard you have a map. The treasure is marked by a cross and the crew even knows the location of the island."

"But I didn't tell a soul," the squire spluttered.

"Somebody's been talking," said the doctor, "never mind who it is."

"Keep that map hidden," whispered the captain.

"I understand," replied Livesey. "We'll make a fort here at the stern of the ship, keeping the weapons and our trusted men close. Do you fear a mutiny, captain?"

"I wouldn't put to sea if I was sure of that, sir. Mr. Arrow and some of the rest of the crew are honest men, I believe. But I want to take every precaution and keep us all safe."

"Well," grunted the squire, "we'll do as you ask, Smollett, but I don't mind telling you I think the worse of you for the things you've said."

"As you please, sir," replied the captain. "You'll see what kind of man I am before long, I've no doubt." He saluted, turned and left us to our thoughts.

By the time we came on deck, the crew were making all the changes Smollett had requested. I was happy to be getting one of the comfy berths at the stern, away from the damp, rocking darkness of the forecastle. The doctor, squire and I, as well as Redruth and the other two servants from the squire's hall, Hunter and Joyce, all had proper beds to sleep in by the main cabin. Captain Smollett and Arrow hung their hammocks in a small hut, or roundhouse, close to the main cabin entrance.

I was exploring the decks and watching the sailors move the rifles and powder when Silver came aboard, climbing up the side of the ship with the agility of a monkey.

"What's all this?" he cried, when he saw the men carrying barrels.

"Captain's orders," called a man.

"But we'll miss the tide if we waste time," Silver protested.

"Get below," boomed the captain, striding across the deck. "Get into your galley and make the men some supper."

"Aye, sir," answered the cook, tapping a finger to the brim of his hat in salute.

"And take this boy with you," called Smollett. He had caught me fiddling with the brass cannon the ship carried, close to the main mast. "I'll have no idlers on my ship."

I hurried after Silver, thinking of what the squire had said about Smollett. He was right, and I hated our captain.

We had a busy time serving the crew food and drinks until dawn, when the mate sounded his whistle and the sailors swarmed onto the rigging. Even though I was almost asleep on my feet, I couldn't leave the deck for my bunk. Everything about the ship getting underway was too exciting. I saw the anchor rise out from the waves and a sailor lashing it to the stern. Next, the sails flapped free and I watched them fill with the breeze.

"Go on, Barbecue," shouted a sailor on the ropes, "give us a song."

"One of the old ones," said another man.

"Ay, mates," Silver called, "it's been a while since you called me by my nickname." He lifted his great head to the sky and sang: "*Fifteen men on the dead man's chest…*"

The whole crew picked up the words: "*Yo, ho, ho, and a bottle of rum!*"

They worked as they sang, and for a second I thought I could hear Billy Bones and his rasping, rum-soaked voice.

After a day or two at sea, the captain's worries about our voyage seemed to have blown away on the ocean winds. The *Hispaniola* was a fine and sturdy ship, and the crew proved their sailing experience.

Not all of Smollett's doubts turned out to be wrong though, as Mr. Arrow began to appear on deck with dull eyes and red cheeks. He often fell or injured himself bumping into things. The captain sent him below decks in disgrace and he would curl up in his bunk and sleep.

We never discovered where he got his drink. The only place onboard where there was a large supply of rum was in the cook's cupboard, but Silver guarded the key like a bear protecting his cave. As the days went by, Arrow got weaker – and drunker – and nobody was very surprised when he vanished one night in a rough sea.

"Fell overboard," growled the captain. "It saves us the trouble of putting him in irons for the rest of the voyage."

We were a man short without Arrow, but Squire Trelawney was a good seaman and he would take a watch on deck. The man who worked the tiller, Israel Hands, was a clever, capable sailor and he took on the rest of the mate's duties. Hands spent much of his free time with Silver, and they seemed to be old friends. But Silver was popular with the whole crew, born to a life at sea. It amazed me to see him move about the ship, steadier and faster than most of the sailors, even when the decks were rolling like the back of a galloping horse.

"He's no ordinary man," Hands told me one night, in the galley. "He had an education, can read any book. And he's brave as a lion. I've seen him take on four men and knock them all down."

Silver was respected and obeyed by the entire crew. With me, he was the kindest master, telling me stories in his neat, swaying galley. His constant companion was Captain Flint, his tropical parrot.

"That bird could be 200 years old," whispered Silver, staring into my eyes. "Nobody's seen so much wickedness. This bird's sailed with the worst cut-throats, from Jamaica to the Indian Ocean.

"Pieces of eight," the parrot screamed – an old pirate cry for a Spanish silver coin.

Long John would feed the parrot cubes of sugar, and I listened in horror as the bird swore oaths when he pulled his hand away.

"You can't be around devils and not get stained a little," grinned Silver.

I knew I was in the company of a fascinating man.

Other people on board were less friendly, and the squire didn't hide the fact that he despised the captain. Smollett admitted to Livesey and me one day that he might have been wrong about the crew. "And the ship's a beauty," he added. "But I still don't like this voyage." The squire heard this and stamped along the deck.

We had some rough weather, but the sailors were happy. The squire gave them double rum rations and sweet pudding at the slightest excuse, and there was always a fresh barrel of red apples open below decks.

"We're spoiling the crew," grumbled Smollett. "Spoil them and they'll turn into devils."

I was glad of that apple barrel as we sailed closer to our island and the days grew hotter. And if it hadn't been for an apple, we might all have had our throats cut…

CHAPTER SEVEN

IN THE BARREL

One evening after sundown, I had decided to go below decks and quench my thirst on an apple. Most of the sailors were gathered at the prow, scanning the horizon for the shape of our island, so nobody was about when I climbed down the ladder. I reached into the barrel – it came up to my chin – but the only fruit left were lying at the bottom, so I swung a leg over and dropped inside. Sitting there in the dark as I chewed my snack, the gentle sway of the waves carried me off to sleep for a few seconds. Suddenly, the wood staves of the barrel rocked as a man slumped down next to it, and I heard a voice, Silver's, rougher than usual.

"Flint was captain," he hissed, "not me. I was in charge of stores after I lost my leg, blown away in the same broadside that tore out Pew's eyes. Flint hired a fancy surgeon to work on my leg."

My blood flashed cold as I listened.

"They were brave and daring, those captains," Silver continued. "I sailed with Captain England first, and then Flint. We made our fortunes, but it's hard to hold onto them. Most of Flint's old boys are on board this ship right now and they were begging in the streets a few weeks ago. Old Pew spent all his gold in one year after Flint died. Then he begged and stole for two years until he was run down in the road."

"That's no life for me," said another voice I recognized as one of the squire's young recruits.

"You're too smart for that," said Silver, coaxingly, "smart as paint."

I shuddered to hear this flattery for it reminded

me how easily the old pirate had won me over.

"You'd succeed as a gentleman of fortune," whispered Silver. "It's a rough life but you'll eat and drink like a king. And when this voyage is over your pockets will be heavy with gold. It's been a good life. I'm fifty now, and when we get back I'll retire to the life of a gentleman. You could do the same."

"But you can't go back to Bristol," said the other man. "You sold your inn, you told me."

"My wife has the money," Silver chuckled. "She'll meet me. I can't say where, as the other men might want to know and I can't trust them as well as I trust you."

"Can you trust her?"

"No man or woman cheats Silver and lives to brag about it. Nobody cheats Barbecue."

"Well, John," said the sailor, "I had my doubts before, but I'm settled now, let's shake on it."

"You're brave and smart," laughed Silver.

I heard another man moving on the stairs and shrank even deeper into the barrel.

"Dick's with us," said Silver.

"He's no fool," answered Israel Hands. "So when do we attack, Silver? I've had enough of this captain, I want to throw him overboard and taste his fine wine."

"You'll stay in the forecastle and be happy eating ship's biscuit until I give the word," snapped Silver. "Smollett pilots the ship for us and the doctor or squire has the map. Let them do the work of finding the treasure for us. Then we strike."

"We don't need Smollett to work the ship," Hands replied, angrily.

"But none of us can plot a course," snapped Silver. "If I had my choice, I'd wait until we were halfway home before we slit their throats, but you and the boys are too impatient for that. We'll finish them when the treasure's aboard. You lot are only happy when you're drunk and soaked in blood, but where does that get you? The hangman's rope, that's where."

"What will you do with the captain and the others?" Dick asked.

"We could maroon them on the island," answered Silver, slyly, "or slice them up."

"That was Billy Bones' way," laughed Hands. "He always said dead men don't bite."

"Death to them," spat Silver. "When we strike, we spare nobody."

"That's my man," growled Hands.

"Now, Dick," said Silver, "all this talk has left me parched. Fetch me an apple."

I could hear Dick rising, coming closer.

"No!" cried Hands. "Let's have some rum instead."

"Take my key, Dick," said Silver, "fill us a jug."

Even in my terror, I began thinking this might be how poor Mr. Arrow got hold of his drink.

"Here's to luck," cried Hands, when Dick had returned with the rum. I could hear them knock together their little tin cups.

"Be patient now and rich later," said Silver.

The next instant, the ship lurched to the side and I heard a shout from the rigging: "Land ho!"

CHAPTER EIGHT

FRIENDS AND ENEMIES

I could hear men rushing about all over the ship. When I was certain that Silver and the others had gone to the open deck, I climbed out of the barrel and ran to the stern deck where I found Hunter and the doctor. I joined them, staring out into the moonlight at two hills shrouded in sea fog.

"Has any man seen this island before?" called the captain.

"I have, sir," answered Silver.

"Is the best place to anchor by that little rock to the south?"

"Yes, captain," said Silver, "the old pirates used to call it Skeleton Island, if the stories are true."

"Steer for that island, Mr. Hands," ordered the captain.

I was desperate to tell my friends everything I'd heard, but knew I must be careful. So I waited until the doctor asked me to fetch his pipe, then tugged at his sleeve.

"I have terrible news," I whispered in his ear. "Get the captain and the squire to the main cabin."

The doctor's eyes flashed, but he remained calm and nodded. He stepped over to the captain and I saw them talking for a moment. Smollett raised his arms and called out: "Lads, all hands on deck!"

I watched as men ran from every corner of the ship.

"You've done the *Hispaniola* proud, lads," said the captain, when the crew had gathered. "The squire, doctor and I must go below decks to plan for landing tomorrow, but I want you to drink our health with a double ration. Rum for all hands!"

The men cheered heartily.

"And a cheer for Captain Smollett," Silver said when the cheer had died down. I could hardly believe this was the same man who wanted us all dead.

"Jim," said Smollett, turning to go below. "I want you down in the cabin too. We might need some writing paper and other supplies."

I joined my friends a minute later. They were seated at the table with a bottle of Spanish wine and a bowl of sweet raisins.

"Let's hear it, Hawkins," the squire commanded.

When I had finished my story the doctor gave me a little cup of wine and filled my palm with raisins. All three men thanked me for my courage.

"I've been a fool," the squire said suddenly, turning to look at the captain. "I am ready to obey your orders."

"No more a fool than I," said Smollett. "I've been tricked too."

"How long will it take for the navy forces at

Bristol to miss us and send a search ship?" asked the doctor.

"Two months at least," sighed the captain.

"Then what is your plan, sir?"

"We must behave as before," said the captain firmly. "We have some time to play with, at least until we find the treasure, but if I ask them to sail away now they'd mutiny at once. I suggest we pick our moment and surprise them with a sudden attack. I will give each of you a small pistol, to keep hidden at all times. Can we trust your servants, squire?"

"As you can trust me."

"Then we are seven, with Hawkins. We don't know how many of the crew are pirates."

"And to think they're all Englishmen," sighed the squire.

"Well, sir," answered the captain, "at least seven of the twenty-six people on this ship are good Englishmen. We must see if we can find some others."

CHAPTER NINE

I GO ASHORE

When I came up on deck the following morning I saw the eastern coast of the island only half a mile distant across the waves. The slopes were covered in thick woods, topped by black rocks and there were streaks of white sand along the shore. I was a little giddy, as the ship was rolling on the waves, and I don't know if it was seasickness or the sight of the island's gloomy forests, but everything about this first look at Treasure Island made my heart sink.

The wind had dropped, so after breakfast the

crew launched our two landing boats and began towing the *Hispaniola* into the shallows between Skeleton Island and the beach of the main island. They grumbled and cursed at their oars while Silver stood with Hands at the wheel, guiding us through the sea passage. He seemed to know the route like the back of his hand. We soon anchored the ship only a few hundred yards from shore, with the grim forest surrounding us on three sides.

A strange smell rolled over the ship, the stench of swamps and rotting leaves. I saw the doctor sniff the air like someone inspecting a bad egg.

"There's fever here," he declared, "I'd stake my wig on it."

The men were restless and bad-tempered when they returned to the ship. They were slow to obey orders and it was clear that mutiny hung over us like a storm cloud. Only Silver seemed cheerful, moving among the sulking sailors and encouraging them to do their work. I was standing close to the squire and doctor, and I heard the captain whisper to them: "Silver wants us to find the treasure before anything happens. Let's try sending the crew ashore. We might be able to capture the ship."

Smollett stepped over to the middle of the deck. "Lads," he called out. "That was hard work rowing us in. The boats are still in the water. You're welcome to go ashore and rest. I'll fire the gun around sundown as a signal for you to return."

The sailors cheered so loudly they startled the birds out of their forest nests. Captain Smollett asked Silver to organize the landing parties, leaving only six men to stay with us on the *Hispaniola*.

I can't explain why, but as Silver arranged the men into groups I had a sudden urge to visit the island myself. Making sure nobody was looking, I slipped into one of the boats and hid under a roll of canvas sail. Part of me knew it was a mad idea, but I thought I might learn something there that would help to save our lives – and I was proved right.

We were halfway to the beach when Silver spotted me from the other boats. "Is that you, Jim?"

he shouted, with a smile. "We can go exploring together. Oh, it's good to be young."

I ignored the old pirate and, as soon as the keel of the boat crunched onto the sand, I jumped out and sprinted for the woods.

I ran until I could run no more. With my lungs bursting for air, I came out into a sandy clearing and wandered between clumps of bright flowers and twisted trees. Here and there I saw snakes, and one even lifted his head from a ledge of rock to hiss at me.

After an hour or more, I came to a grove of oaks, with their roots twisting over the sand like giant brambles. Beyond the trees I could see a swamp, covered in mist. I heard voices rolling out of this mist and quickly hid myself behind a rotting log.

Silver and another man stepped out of the grove, deep in conversation.

"Tom, mate," said Silver, softly. "I'm trying to protect you. We can't change what's happened."

"Long John," cried the other man, close to

despair, "I've heard you're honest. Answer me true, why are you running with these mutinous dogs?"

There was a sudden scream from far off in the woods. It echoed around the swamps until only the murmur of the distant surf disturbed the silence of the clearing. Silver didn't blink an eye at this terrible sound.

"Please, Barbecue…" pleaded Tom, and he stretched out a hand.

"Hands off," snapped Silver, swinging backwards on his crutch.

"What was that noise?" asked Tom desperately, like a drowning man reaching for help.

"That must have been Alan," said Silver, his eyes as still and cold as glass.

"Alan?" Tom cried, in a sudden fury. "Then he was a true and honest seaman. I'll die like Alan before I join any mutiny. Kill me too, if you can, but I'm turning you down."

This brave man turned his back on the cook and walked away. Silver bellowed in rage and I watched him throw his crutch like a spear. It struck Tom point-first in his back and the poor sailor gasped and fell to the ground. Silver sprang across the clearing like a monkey and buried his knife in his victim. I was close enough to hear him wheezing for breath as he jabbed at the corpse.

The murderer retrieved his crutch, took a whistle from his pocket and blew a high note three times. I guessed this must be a signal for the other pirates and knew I must escape before they arrived. Already, I could hear a chorus of shrieks erupt from the thick forest. I crept away from the log and started running, almost blind with fear. Crashing through the woods, I finally stopped and looked around to get my bearings. My blood ran cold as I saw a flicker, a dark shape in the trees just ahead.

I couldn't tell what kind of strange beast it was but the sight filled me with terror. It was moving stooped over on two legs, like some type of man, maybe a savage or cannibal? I turned to retreat, but the creature quickly blocked me and I realized that

I might have to fight for my life. It was then that I remembered the little pistol the captain had given me, and I snatched it from my pocket.

"Who are you?" I demanded, approaching the figure with my pistol.

"Ben Gunn," answered a dry, crackling voice. The scruffiest man I have ever seen stepped out from behind a tree. He was clothed in a crazy patchwork of animal skins and twigs, and his hair was so long and knotted it looked like animal fur.

"Were you shipwrecked here?" I asked, in wonder.

"Worse," he chuckled. "Marooned, left with no food or supplies except a pistol with a single shot. I've been here three years, eating berries and nuts. A man can survive anywhere but there are things he misses. Do you have any cheese?"

"Cheese?" I asked in amazement.

"A single piece? I dream of it all the time."

"If I ever get back to my ship, I'll give you more cheese than you can carry."

"What's your name?" he asked, slyly. "And what's stopping you from getting to your ship?"

"My name's Jim."

"Jim," he sighed. "I was a good boy like you, Jim, when I was growing up, but I took to gambling and ended up here. I've had time to think. I'm going to lead a good life when I get home. And Jim," he whispered, glancing around at the trees, "I'm rich as a king, you know."

He squealed and raised his hands in protest when he saw my expression. After years alone on the island, he was clearly mad.

"I can make you rich too," he laughed. "But business first. That isn't Flint's ship in the bay, is it?"

"Flint's dead," I told him. "Some of his men aren't, though, I'm afraid."

"Is there a chief among them," he hissed, "with only one leg?"

I nodded and Ben Gunn snatched my wrist and pulled me close.

"Oh, he's terrible," he whispered, his eyes very wide. "You've not joined with him, have you?"

I quickly explained how we had come to the island, describing some of the horrors I had seen.

"Would your squire take me home?" asked Ben Gunn, stroking his furry chin.

"He's a gentleman. I am sure he would."

"Well, I was here with Flint, that's my story. He went off with six strong men and all the gold while we waited on the *Walrus*, his ship. Flint came back alone, and you know what that means. Billy Bones and Silver wanted to know where the treasure was, but Flint only laughed and said the *Walrus* was setting sail. So I came back to the island on another ship, much later, and told that crew about the treasure. We dug for twelve days, we found nothing, and each day they hated me more. When we got back to the ship, they said I could stay here digging, and they left me here."

He pinched my wrist and gave me an odd smile. "I'm no fool, though," he tittered. "You tell the squire I'm the man for him."

"I don't understand you, but it doesn't matter, because I can't speak to the squire. I can't get back to the ship."

"I have a boat!" Ben Gunn said, with a whoop of excitement. "She's hidden below the white rock."

The boom of a cannon shot rolled around the hills.

"They're fighting," I shouted. "Come on."

We rushed through the woods, heading towards the sound of rifle shots. I could see a Union Jack flag fluttering over the treetops.

CHAPTER TEN

THE DOCTOR TAKES OVER

At this point in my story, I must ask the doctor to describe what happened on the *Hispaniola* in my absence. He has kindly sent me this letter, with all the vital facts:

Well, Jim, we would have attacked the six pirates that Silver left on board with us, to capture the ship, but we had to wait for a wind to sail to the open sea and then Hunter broke the news that you were missing! After searching the ship, I told the squire I must go to the island to find you with Hunter, and I set out in a small rowing boat. There is a fort marked on Flint's map and we decided to try there first, thinking you might be taking shelter.

We could see Silver's two landing boats tied up by the swamp, each with a lookout. They waved their arms and shouted when they saw us, but they stayed where they were and didn't run to raise the alarm.

When we reached the shore, I charged into the forest and didn't stop until I came up to the fence that runs all around the fort. Flint and his men had done a good job. The pirates had constructed a log house around a spring of clean water, with a large main room and gun slits in every wall. They had cleared all the trees around the log house and used them to build the fence, six-feet high and spiked at the top. If the defenders had enough food and weapons they could hold this place against an army.

It was a joy to find the spring. We had plenty of arms, fine wines and fancy foods on the Hispaniola but no water. Hunter and I were laughing at this good discovery when we heard a scream from the woods, and I confess that my first thought was: "Jim Hawkins is no more."

But doctors cannot afford to let their feelings delay their actions. We hurried back to the ship, to report everything we'd found. The squire greeted us on the deck, his face white as chalk.

"I'm to blame if the lad's hurt," he told me, "I brought us all to this terrible place."

"Never mind that, squire," the captain interrupted. "I heard the other sailors arguing when that scream came across the water, so some might still be loyal to the ship. We can't sail her with no wind or crew to tow her, though. We'll be safer at the fort."

We acted quickly. Redruth guarded the passageway from the main cabin to the forecastle, while Hunter brought the rowing boat around to the stern. There was a wide window in the main cabin and we started loading the boat with gunpowder, arms, cognac, biscuits and my trusty medicine bag. While we prepared for the escape, the captain went to speak to Israel Hands.

"Sailor," called the captain, in a hard, icy voice. "We have pistols and rifles and if any man tries to signal to shore we'll shoot him dead."

Hands and the rest of the crew dropped through the deck hatches and I could hear rushing feet inside the ship. When they met Redruth waiting in the passage with four loaded rifles they tried to climb back onto the deck.

"Down, you dogs," shouted the captain.

The squire and captain guarded the six sailors while the rest of us made a trip to the island in the rowing boat, ferrying our supplies to the stockade. I left Joyce and Hunter there while I rowed back to the Hispaniola.

The squire was waiting for me at the main cabin window, his expression fiercer and more determined than ever. We loaded the boat and took more muskets and cutlasses for the squire, the captain, Redruth and myself. I tipped the rest of the ships' arms overboard and allowed myself a grin when I saw the bright steel glinting far below the waves.

When everything was ready for us to depart, the captain rushed up to the forecastle hatch.

"Is there any good man who wants to join us?" he shouted. "Are you still loyal to me, sailor Abraham?"

There was a shout and the sound of blows and then Abraham burst into the sunlight with a fresh gash across his cheek.

"I'm with you, sir," he cried.

We crowded into the boat and started for shore. With Abraham and all the arms we were badly overloaded, but this was the least of our worries. I saw Smollett glance back to the ship. "The gun," he whispered, almost to himself. "We forgot about the cannon."

I looked behind us and saw the five pirates on the deck turning the cannon. We hadn't thought of sinking the balls or powder for this terrible weapon.

"Hands was Flint's gunner," choked Abraham.

"Keep rowing," barked the captain, coming to his senses. "Who's the best shot here?"

"Mr. Trelawney," I replied.

"Squire," said the captain in a calm voice, "see if you can hit that rascal Hands for us."

I watched the squire load a musket with hands as steady as steel. Hands was working at the front of the cannon, but he ducked down to fetch something at the same instant the squire fired. One of the other men around the gun howled and toppled over.

There was a yell from the island and I saw a group of pirates rush across the sand to the two boats.

"Here they come," I cried. "They'll try to cut us off from landing at the fort beach."

"We'll beat them to it," cried the captain. "The cannon's the worry. They're firing."

We yanked on the oars to try to turn the boat. I heard a crunch and boom and could sense the cannonball streaking over our heads. Hands had missed but we were sinking. Too heavy for any sudden movement, our boat sank in three feet of water, close to the shore. Most of the stores were ruined.

"Save what you can," ordered the captain, "and run for the fort."

I could hear shouts from the woods as the other pirates landed. A branch cracked nearby as they raced to catch us.

"Give Trelawney the loaded muskets," I told the captain. I saw that Abraham was unarmed and I passed him my cutlass. He spat in his hands and sliced the sword through the air, making me feel he might be worth his salt in any battle to come.

We reached the fence first, on the south side. Seven pirates rushed around from the west, but we managed to let off four shots – two from our friends in the log house – before they saw us. They darted back into the trees, leaving one man dead behind.

I was about to let out a whoop at this easy victory when I heard a crack from the trees and poor Redruth tumbled over. I could see he was finished but we carried him over the fence, bleeding and groaning. Not once had this loyal servant complained, even with all the dangers we'd put him through. We laid him down gently in the log house and the squire kneeled by his side, blubbing like a baby.

"You're going home," I told the dying man.

"Forgive me," begged the squire.

"That's not proper," Redruth whispered, "not between a servant and his squire, but of course I do."

He was dead in a minute. When I staggered out into the fort clearing, to find and help the captain, I saw him fixing a long pole to the log house. He ran up a Union Jack flag that he'd hidden in his tunic. The next instant, the air shook and a cannonball screamed over the log house to go crashing into the trees.

"Blaze away, Hands," cried the captain. "See if we care."

"You can't see the fort from the ship," I shouted. "He's aiming for your flag. Wouldn't it be wiser to lower it?"

"Lower my flag, sir?" glowered the captain. "Never."

All through the afternoon they blasted away at us, but could never find their target. Smollett used the hours to examine our stores carefully.

"We've food for ten days," he announced. "There are six of us to fight, one man's dead and one cabin boy's missing."

There was a shout from Hunter, who was keeping lookout at the door.

"Jim's not missing, captain," laughed Hunter, "he's climbing over the fence."

Back to you now, Jim…

David Livesey, Ship's Doctor

CHAPTER ELEVEN

CUTLASS AND PISTOL

The second Ben Gunn saw the fluttering Union Jack, he knew my friends had taken the fort.

"No honest pirate would fly that flag," he laughed. "They'd pick the Jolly Roger. There's been a fight, I'll bet, and your friends are safe inside."

"We must join them," I cried, stepping forward, but Ben Gunn didn't move.

"You know where to find me," he whispered, "or send one of your friends. But tell them to carry a white cloth as a sign of peace. We don't want any accidents."

He tapped a pocket and I guessed he had a knife or pistol hidden in there.

"I'll do as you say," I told him. "Do you have any other message for them?"

"Only that they've got a lot to gain," he answered, mysteriously, "by making friends with Ben Gunn. And if you happen to meet Silver, you won't mention me, will you, lad?"

"Of course not."

"I knew it. You see, if those pirates camp in the woods tonight, there'll be some new widows in England by the morning."

I didn't understand a word of this, but before I could ask him anything else, the wild man had scampered into the woods, whistling and laughing to himself.

It took me more than an hour to move slowly through the forest, keeping a watch for any pirate patrols. I came to a clearing on the hill and from there I could see the *Hispaniola* lying at anchor. Just as Ben Gunn had predicted, the sinister Jolly

Roger flag was flying from her main mast.

Down at the shore, a group of pirates were dragging the sunken rowing boat from the water. I watched them chop at it with axes and, when I looked further along the beach, I saw a great bonfire was already starting to burn where they were making their camp. In the twilight gloom, the trees flickered with orange and red light. I heard the pirates singing and shouting, and guessed that they'd already been supping at Silver's tub of rum.

As I crept closer to the fort, I noticed a crag of rock sticking out from the tall trees. It was close to the shore and white as the moon and I wondered if Ben Gunn's ramblings about a secret boat had been true. I tried to remember the position of this crag as I stumbled into the rough posts of the fence.

My friends gave me a warm welcome and after I'd told them all my news, I made myself as comfortable as I could in the rough log house. A sharp evening breeze whistled through the cracks in the walls and it was impossible to keep grains of blowing sand out of my eyes, my teeth and every mouthful of food. To make matters worse, our chimney was a hole in the roof and most of the smoke from our fire stayed inside.

My eyes were streaming and I was very cold, but there was no time to sit around feeling sorry for myself. Captain Smollett soon had me on guard duty at the door to the open clearing, while the doctor did the cooking. Meanwhile, some of the men went looking for firewood, whilst others dug a grave for poor Redruth.

"Jim," said the doctor, coming out of the smoky interior for a breath of fresh air. "Do you think this Ben Gunn is completely mad?"

"Hard to say, sir," I replied.

"He wanted cheese?"

"Yes, sir."

"Mad or not, I share his passion for cheese. You've seen the little box I have for tobacco, Jim?"

I nodded, although I was very puzzled.

"But that's not where I keep my tobacco," the doctor went on, mysteriously. "No, I keep a piece of parmesan cheese in there, and nothing else. That piece of cheese is for Ben Gunn, if he'll help us. Let's hope it's enough to win him over."

We buried Redruth before sitting down for dinner. It was a glum meal, with a cup of brandy and a boiled pork chop for each man. When they'd finished eating, the doctor, squire and captain went to a corner of the room and discussed our chances of survival.

"We'll starve before any rescue boat gets here," whispered the captain.

"Then we'll have to fight for the ship," the squire said. "There are only fifteen of them left now, by my count."

"And the man you shot at the cannon," added the doctor. "I imagine he's under the waves by now. That's fourteen."

"The squire's good aim might save us yet," smiled the captain.

"And we have two other weapons," said the doctor. "Rum and fever."

We could all hear the pirates, drunk and roaring by the bonfire on the edge of the swamp.

"Half of them will be too sick to walk before the end of the week," laughed the doctor.

"If we can't beat them, we'll force them to sail away on the ship," said the squire.

"It's the first ship I've lost," the captain whispered, sadly.

I could hear them talking softly after this, but was too tired to keep my eyes open and their words soon faded into my dreams. When I woke, the glaring sun was hot on my face. A man was at the door shouting: "Two pirates, and they're waving a white flag."

I ran to a gun slit and saw Silver and another man waiting on the far side of the fence.

"Keep your distance, Long John," shouted the captain. "Or we fire."

"Captain Silver has only come to talk and

discuss terms," the other pirate protested.

"He's *captain* now, is he?" laughed Smollett.

"The crew elected me," said Silver, meekly, "after you deserted the ship, sir. Can I have safe passage into the stockade?"

"There's nothing to discuss," Smollett growled. "But enter if you wish."

Silver tossed his crutch over the fence and swung himself over quick as a cat. He was slower on the sloping sand of the clearing, though. As he came closer, I saw that he'd changed into a fine blue suit dotted with brass buttons, and he wore a laced hat.

"We'll talk out here," said Smollett, blocking the door.

"Won't you ask me in, captain?" asked Silver.

"Out here," the captain repeated. Silver grumbled but he dropped his crutch and sank to the ground. "Morning to you, Jim," he called out, when he saw me watching. I didn't return his greeting.

"Well," he began, "that was a neat trick last night with the club. Some of my people were badly shaken by it. But don't try it again, by thunder," he suddenly snarled. "I wasn't drunk like the others and I almost caught you. My man was still alive when I got to him."

Had Ben Gunn been stalking through the pirate camp?

"Is that all?" asked Smollett, showing no reaction to what Silver had told him.

"If you want to live," Silver continued, "give me the map. My crew will attack if you don't, and I never wanted that. I'll promise you safe passage in the *Hispaniola*, after we've loaded the treasure, to any port you choose, if you give me the map. That's a rare deal for you, Captain Smollett."

"Anything else to say, Silver?" asked our captain.

"If you refuse," Silver snapped, "you've seen the last of me but musket balls and the sharp edge of a sword."

"Then hear me," replied the captain. "Give

yourselves up and I'll promise you a fair trial in England. If not, my name is Alexander Smollett, I've hoisted my king's flag and I'll see you in hell before I surrender."

Silver's whole face twitched in fury. He let out a stream of terrible oaths that made me shudder, and dragged himself up from the ground.

"Those that die quickly will be the lucky ones," he told us, before stumbling away down the slope.

"To your posts," cried our captain.

He paced around the room, checking our rifles and stores of gunpowder.

"Keep steady, lads," he told us, "don't let them get too close to the gun slits."

The next second my ears were ringing as a volley of shots broke from every side of the fort. I heard several musket balls slam into the walls and then there was a fearsome roar from the north fence, as a band of pirates swarmed over the posts. The room filled with smoke as our men fired and I saw three pirates knocked to the ground. Four others were dashing across the clearing, waving pistols and swords. They screamed a war cry that was echoed by their mates with guns in the forest.

"Cut at 'em," screamed one of the attackers, rushing into the log house. He sent Hunter crashing to the floor with a single blow. Another pirate started hacking at the doctor with a cutlass and the captain cried: "Out lads, fight them in the open."

I grabbed a sword and ran into the daylight. The doctor was ahead of me, chasing after the man who had attacked him. With one mighty sweep of his blade, the doctor sent the man rolling down the hill. I rushed around the log house and came face to face with a huge pirate, lifting his rusty cutlass over his head so it glinted in the sun. There was no time to think or be afraid. I dodged to the side, lost my footing and fell. I looked up, thinking this might be my last moment on earth, but saw Abraham sink his cutlass into the pirate's broad chest.

"Get inside," called the doctor. Abraham helped me up and we dashed into the shelter of the log house. Hunter was lying on the ground, too stunned to move, and poor Joyce had been shot through the head. In the middle of the log house, the captain was leaning heavily on the squire.

"Here's a brave wounded man, lads," said the squire.

"Have they run away?" asked Smollett.

"Those that can still run," answered the doctor.

"That's fine," said the captain. "The odds are improving for us, gentlemen."

CHAPTER TWELVE

I BOARD THE HISPANIOLA

We had paid a hard price for our victory at the fort. The captain had been shot twice, in the shoulder and the leg – though the doctor said he would recover – and poor Hunter's chest was so badly crushed he was as good as dead.

Silver's pirates must have been nursing their wounds in the swamps, because we heard nothing from them all morning. After a lunch of pork ribs and beans, Smollett and Livesey retreated to a corner and spoke in whispers. The doctor finally stood, picked up his hat and strapped his sword belt around his waist. He took two pistols and a musket and set off across the clearing to disappear over the fence.

"Has Mr. Livesey gone mad?" Abraham asked.

"I doubt it," I replied. "I think he's off to meet a certain Ben Gunn."

The day wore on, getting hotter with every minute and I soon envied the doctor his walk through the cool glades of the forest. The longer I spent at my tiresome chores, the more I dreamed of escaping the heat and glare of the fort. I found myself filling my pockets with apples, biscuits and two more pistols, supplies for another of my solo adventures. The captain would never give me permission to leave the fort, but I was determined to find out if Ben Gunn was telling the truth about his secret boat. I would slip away while the others were resting and hoped to return before they'd noticed I was gone.

When Abraham and the squire got ready to change the bandage on the captain's leg, I saw my chance. I made a bolt for the fence and a moment later I was picking my way through the thick forest.

It took me at least an hour to reach the base of the white crag, and night was coming down quickly. I soon found an oar and a little cup of a boat hidden behind some bushes. It looked almost like a round bathtub made of sticks and goatskins, and was so roughly built I could hardly believe it would float.

I had planned to return to the fort once I'd checked to see if the boat was really there, but the sight of it gave me a fresh idea. If I could reach the *Hispaniola*, under cover of darkness and sea fog, I could cut her anchor rope and she would drift onto the shore and be ruined. Without their ship, the pirates would be forced to make peace with Captain Smollett until a rescue party arrived.

I didn't stop for a second to worry that my plan was dangerous. Instead, I lifted the boat over my head and staggered between the trees to the breaking surf.

For all its rough and ready looks, Ben Gunn's boat was a safe and sturdy craft. She floated well and, as luck would have it, the falling tide carried me out to the blinking lanterns of the *Hispaniola*. I was soon bobbing under the anchor rope and had my knife ready to cut the ship loose. But, when I reached up to touch the line with my fingertips, I realized it was stretched tight.

An old sailor at the Admiral Benbow had once told me that when a cable snaps it can kick like a frightened horse. So I decided it would be safer to wait until the ship turned on the breeze and the rope went slack before I tried to cut through it. Before long, I heard the sails flapping and the rope dipped into the water. I lunged forwards and started sawing with my knife until there were only two, thin strands of rope left holding the thick line together.

I was getting ready to cut the last strands when I heard shouts from the main cabin window above my head. Two men were arguing, drunk on rum no doubt, and I recognized one of the voices as belonging to Israel Hands.

Wasting no more time, I cut through the last ties and the *Hispaniola* lurched to the side. My little boat was swept along the hull and I was startled when something soft brushed over my hand. It was a rope, trailing from the deck.

With no plan in my head, I took hold of the rope and floated along with the drifting ship. Again, I heard shouts from the cabin, and when I pulled on the rope I found I could stand in my little boat and peep through the open window. I was amazed to see Hands and the other sailor rolling and crashing about the room, locked together in deadly combat. Both men were red-faced and panting, slashing at each other with knives.

My only thought was to get away. I dropped back into my boat, ready to push off, but the stray rope I had found was tangled around my oar and I wasted a minute or two unpicking it. When I had finished and looked around to get my bearings, my heart rushed into my mouth with shock. The *Hispaniola* had turned on the current. Instead of drifting towards the beach, she was rushing past the end of Skeleton Island. I was being pulled along with her on the waves, out into the ocean.

I heard a scream from inside the ship, but was too frozen with fear to glance up to the deck. The rollers were getting larger as we approached the open sea. My fragile craft was bucking and swaying so much I was afraid of toppling over the side. I could only curl up in a ball inside my cup of hides and sticks, expecting a watery death at any second. I must have lain like this for hours, but eventually, overwhelmed by exhaustion, I fell asleep, and dreamed of dry land and my dear old Admiral Benbow.

I woke in daylight, soaking wet, and weary. To my great relief, I saw I was only a quarter mile off Treasure Island, around at its southwestern tip. There were huge, breaking waves along the shore here, but I remembered from Flint's map that there were open and safe beaches on the west and north coast of the island. I tried my best to steer Ben Gunn's bathtub with my little oar and went skimming along over the mounds of blue water and white foam.

I was rapidly floating westwards when I saw a shining flash of white sails ahead of me – it was the *Hispaniola*. Fearing the pirates had spotted me, I watched as the ship came on with full sails and then veered suddenly off to one side, rolling about on the swell. She repeated this motion several times until I guessed the truth – that there was nobody at the tiller steering her. After I cut the ship loose, Hands and the other man must have deserted her. I almost cried with joy when I realized I might be able to board the ship and somehow return her to her rightful captain, Mr. Smollett.

I must have been half-mad from thirst and the baking sun as I paddled desperately toward the ship. When I had closed the gap to one hundred yards, I saw the ship suddenly turn again. Her prow sliced through the waves, rushing in my direction. I found myself riding on top of one wave with the *Hispaniola* looming above me on the next, and made a wild leap for some ropes hanging from the ship's figurehead. As I caught hold of the line and scrambled up, I heard a crunch. My little boat vanished under the ship. There was no going back.

I had thought the ship was deserted, but I soon came across the two pirate watchmen I'd seen fighting the night before. Hands was slumped across the deck, his back resting against a barrel. His face was as white and greasy as candlewax and there was a pool of blood around his legs. The other man lay nearby, stiff and dead, his lips drawn back over his teeth in a horrible snarl.

Hands' eyes rolled open. "Brandy," he hissed.

This was the same man who had tried to blow my friends out of the water with the cannon, but even so I could not stand idle and watch him suffer.

I ran down to the cabin and foraged in the cupboards until I found a brandy bottle and some food for my aching stomach, then returned to the injured man.

"That's good medicine," growled Hands, when he'd swigged a good third of the brandy. "I'm just unlucky the doctor's not here to stitch me up. But I'm not as unlucky as him," and he waved the bottle towards the man he had killed.

"I'm taking command of the ship, Mr. Hands," I announced proudly. "You can call me captain."

My first act was to walk over to the main mast, lower the Jolly Roger and toss it overboard.

"Well, Captain," sneered Hands, "how are you going to sail her? If you fetch me some food and bandages for my wounds, I'll teach you how it's done."

I had no choice but to accept his offer. When the deep cuts in his body were all bound up, Hands showed me how to fix a simple sail and steer the ship into the wind.

"You're doing a fine job, Captain," joked Hands. "But I'm almost passing out with thirst and the brandy is too strong for me. Would you be a saint and go below deck to fetch me some cool wine?"

It was clear to me that Hands was plotting something. I'd already seen him glugging the brandy as though it was water. However, I wanted to find out what he was up to, so I played along with his request.

"I'll be a few minutes," I called, and hurried down the ladder to the main cabin. I quickly kicked off my shoes and tiptoed along to the forecastle hatch and stuck my head out an inch or two. Hands dragged himself over to a coil of rope and picked out a jagged knife, still red with blood. I saw him hide the weapon in his jacket and then crawl back to the barrel.

Sneaking back down the passageway, I tried my best to hide my fears as I climbed up to the deck with his wine bottle. I guessed that Hands would want my help getting the *Hispaniola* to shore, so I thought I would be safe at least until we reached dry land.

For the next hour, we carefully guided the ship towards a wide stretch of beach.

"We're not the first to try it," cried Hands, "I can see another ship there."

I looked closely and spotted an old wreck on the beach, all covered in seaweed and forest creepers.

"We can pull up alongside," he laughed.

"But how do we get her off the sand?" I asked.

"With a rope and a pulley and a good heave. Now bring in that sail."

Hands had me rushing around the deck with his orders, pulling ropes and dropping the sail. The ship hissing through the shallow water and I glanced down at the beach rushing towards us. A shadow flickered on the waves below me and when I spun around I saw Hands towering over me with his knife held high. He roared like a bull and charged at me, but his wounds made him slow and I easily outpaced him. I snatched one of my pistols from a pocket, aimed and pulled the trigger. The hammer clicked down, but there was no flash or explosion.

"Wet powder," laughed Hands, lumbering towards me. "And nowhere to run."

The next second, the *Hispaniola* crunched into the sand and we were both thrown across the deck. I was up on my feet first, climbing into the nets of the rigging until I reached a small, wooden perch, thirty feet above the deck. I carefully checked my last two loaded pistols, all the time watching Hands. He cursed his bad luck, fixed the knife between his teeth and started up the rigging to get to me.

"One step closer, Mr. Hands," I warned him, "and I'll blow your brains out." I had both my pistols aimed at his forehead.

Hands took the knife in one hand so he could talk. "Jim," he appealed, "let's make peace."

I hardly noticed his hand reaching back over his shoulder. The knife sang through the air like an arrow and I felt a stab of pain in my shoulder as the blade pinned me to the mast. My fingers must have trembled with the shock, as both my pistols fired and Hands crashed into the water.

When I'd caught my breath I looked down and saw Hands' body lying on the bright sand of the shallows. He had drowned, food for the fishes, in the very spot he'd planned to slaughter me.

CHAPTER THIRTEEN

IN THE PIRATES' DEN

With a wrench of my body, Hands' knife broke free and I was able to climb down to the deck. I quickly bandaged my wound and found some fresh water to drink. It was already dusk by the time I was feeling strong enough to go in search of my friends. The moon was high in the night sky when I finally reached the rough poles of our fort.

I climbed the fence in silence, not wanting to be shot by mistake as an intruder. My friends were snoring away in the log house as I tiptoed in.

I planned to lie down in my usual place and let them discover me in the morning, but as I stretched out a hand I heard a screech and a terrifying cry: "Pieces of eight!"

"Who goes there?" shouted Silver, woken by his parrot. I tried to run, but his hand snaked out and held my wrist in a steel grip. The pirates had taken our fort.

Silver lit a torch and I looked quickly around the log house. I could see no sign of my friends, but there were six men with Silver, one of them badly injured.

"Shiver me timbers," cried Silver. "It's my friend, Jim."

Silver sat down heavily on a barrel while the other pirates circled around me, muttering curses.

"I like you, Jim," Silver continued. "You remind me of my young self. I'm glad you're joining our company. The captain was very disappointed when you deserted and the doctor even called you a scamp, but I say you're welcome."

"But what happened here?" I asked him. "Where are my friends?"

"When we saw the ship was gone we made a bargain," Silver explained. "We got the fort and they were free to go, though the doctor promised he'd visit to treat the wounded and sick. We won't bother them now. So, are you joining up with us, Jim?"

"Never," I said. "And you might as well know it was me that took Billy Bones' map, me that heard you plotting and warned the captain, me who took the ship away from you. I don't care if you kill me or not, but if you spare me I'll try my best to save you from the rope when you stand trial for mutiny."

The pirates stared at me in silent amazement, until one of them pulled a knife from his belt. "I'll deal with him, lads," he cried.

"Step away," shouted Silver, holding my attacker back with his crutch. "I'm captain here."

"And we're tired of it," shouted another man.

"Let's see one of you face me with a cutlass," Silver challenged them.

Not one of them moved.

"Then obey me," snapped Silver. "Nobody touches the boy."

"This crew's got rights," said the man with the knife. "I want a meeting."

"A meeting?" laughed Silver.

"A private meeting," answered the man. "Outside."

The men hurried to the door and when they were all gone Silver leaned close to my ear. "Jim," he pleaded, "you're in terrible danger. I'll do what I can to save you, but we have to be in this together, fighting back to back to save our lives. Will you try to help me, like you said you would?"

"I will."

"I'm on the squire's side again," he whispered, with a smile. "I know when I'm beaten. But what puzzles me, Jim, is if they knew they'd won, why did the doctor and the squire give me Flint's map."

I could only shrug and shake my head as the

six pirates returned in silence. One man stepped forwards and reached a hand out to pass something to Silver.

"The Black Spot," hissed Silver, staring into his palm. "What does it say on the back? 'Captain no more.' Well, I have a right to defend myself. What are your claims?"

"You've made a bad job of it, Silver," one of the men cried. "You let the enemy go and wouldn't let us attack them when they were out in the woods. And now this boy's turned up, and taken our ship."

"I didn't want to rush things," Silver protested, "I wanted to wait. You forced me to act and that's why all our plans went wrong. And this boy is our hostage, I didn't want you to kill our only hostage, lads."

"Why did you let the others go then?" asked one of the men.

"For this," cried Silver, triumphantly. He pulled the map from his long coat and dropped it to the dirt floor.

"It's really Flint's," cried a man, dropping to his knees to examine the map.

"What good is gold if we've no ship?" another pirate complained.

"Let's start with the treasure," replied Silver. "We'll find the ship when we need it."

"Barbecue for captain," shouted one of the men.

"Aye," said the man with the knife, "let's stick with Long John."

"That's the way, lads," shouted Long John. "And tomorrow we'll find the treasure and every one of us will be rich."

CHAPTER FOURTEEN

THE TREASURE HUNT

I woke to hear Silver welcoming someone into the log house. "Good morning, sir," Silver purred. "We've got a new lodger, a little stranger."

"Jim?" gasped Dr. Livesey. For a second, he looked amazed, but then he gave me a nod and hurried over to treat the wounded pirate. The doctor's bravery was incredible. He moved among the sailors, checking them for fever and handing out pills as though he was out visiting his country patients.

When he had finished, he turned to Silver and

said casually: "I should like to talk with the boy. I'll wait at the fence."

The mood in the log house changed in a flash. The pirates all glared at me as the doctor stepped out. "Not one word," said a man in the corner.

"Silence," growled Silver. "Will you swear to die if you betray us and run, Jim?"

"I will."

"The doctor has stuck with the deal we made," said Silver, glancing around the log house. "In return for his kindness, I'll let him talk with the boy. I'll keep close to them, lads, don't you worry."

Silver led me across the clearing to the waiting doctor. I could hear the pirates in the log house behind us grumbling, but none of them followed.

"I saved the boy," Silver whispered to the doctor, making sure the pirates couldn't see him talking. "I risked everything to do it, remember that before you judge me."

The old pirate hobbled a few yards to sit down on a tree stump and waved a hand to the watching pirates. "And be quick about it," he told us.

"Jim, how could you run off and leave us?" the doctor asked me, wasting no time. "It was cowardly."

I let out a sob and tears welled in my eyes. "Forgive me," I begged. "I didn't mean to abandon you. I wanted to get you the ship."

"The ship?" said the doctor, hardly believing his ears.

"I've beached her, sir, and only I know where."

"Then you've saved our lives, again," he replied. "And we'll save you, Jim."

"Time's up," called Silver, loud enough for the other pirates to hear. He swung himself over and took my arm.

"Silver," the doctor whispered, "don't be in a hurry to go looking for treasure."

"Jim and I are dead men if we delay," answered Silver.

"Then look out for storms and thunder when you find it," said the doctor, mysteriously. "If you get Jim out of this wolf trap, I'll do my best to help you in any court of law.

The doctor nodded to Silver, shook my hand and darted into the woods.

We left the camp an hour later, with each of the six pirates carrying shovels and guns, and Silver leading me along on a rope tied around my waist, like a dancing bear. A short march found us on the slopes of the hill that crowned the island, searching for the tall tree marked on Flint's map.

The going was hard for Silver and we were struggling to keep up with the others when we heard a cry of terror. When we reached the man who had given the shout, we saw a skeleton stretched out at the base of a great pine tree. There were shreds of cloth draped around the bones – sailor's clothes.

"Why's he laid out like that?" asked one of the pirates.

The dead man's arms were arranged above his skull with its gaping eye sockets, pointing in a line.

"It's a marker," hissed Silver. "A compass to show us the way."

"It's ghostly," said one of the men, "that's what it is. This place is haunted."

"Get moving," growled Silver. "Flint's dead, boys. He can't hurt us and I want his doubloons."

The pirates stayed closer together in a group as we started up the hill. A thin, trembling voice suddenly called out from the woods behind us:

"Fifteen men on the dead man's chest,

Yo, ho, ho and a bottle of rum!"

The pirates screamed in wild panic. "It's Flint," yelled the man who had passed Silver the Black Spot.

"It's a prank," answered Silver, trying to keep his voice steady. The voice in the woods called again: "Fetch me my rum, Darby McGraw..."

"Those were Flint's last words," sobbed one of the pirates. "Only his ghost would know that."

I saw Silver gritting his teeth together, mastering his fear. "I'll shake my fist in Flint's dead face," he roared, "to get my hands on that treasure. But wait," he asked suddenly, "did that voice remind you of another man, lads?"

"Another pirate, yes," said the man the doctor had bandaged that morning. "I recognize it. There was a sailor…"

"Ben Gunn!" cried Silver. "It sounds more like him than Flint. Ben went missing years ago. Maybe he ended up here. I fear Ben Gunn less than I fear a fly."

The pirates started to laugh and cheer. They were back on the treasure hunt, keener than ever.

We followed the direction of the skeleton marker until we reached three giant trees close to the summit of the hill. Silver checked the map and pointed to the middle tree. He let out a howl that chilled my blood and then yanked on my rope, turning to give me an awful scowl. He was a fierce pirate again, mad with excitement to be so close to Flint's gold. We were only ten paces from the location of the treasure and the pirates ran forward like hounds baying for blood.

I heard a yell and Silver dragged me through some thick bushes to the edge of a giant pit. It was empty, with bare dirt sides and only some broken bits of wood lying at the bottom. The *Walrus* had been branded into one cracked board with a red-hot iron. Flint's treasure was long gone.

CHAPTER FIFTEEN

THE CAPTAIN VANISHES

"We've been robbed," cried a pirate. "Silver's tricked us."

Silver passed me a pistol behind his back.

"He must be working for the squire," another said. "Let's finish him and the scamp."

I watched the furious pirates lifting their guns, but before they could shoot, shots exploded all around us. Three of the men toppled into the pit. The others ran for cover in the woods.

The doctor, Abraham and Ben Gunn sprang from the bushes, with smoke still curling from their muskets.

"Just in time," laughed Silver. "And you, Ben Gunn... so I was right about you being the ghost."

"It was all his plan," said the doctor. "He stumbled across the skeleton a year after he was left here alone, and followed the clue to the tall tree. The grass was a different length over the pit so he knew where to dig. When he told me he'd moved the treasure to the cave he calls home, I knew Flint's map was worthless."

"So you gave it to me to make your bargain," chuckled Silver.

"Yes, and we all moved to the cave, which is more comfortable than the fort, I'm glad to say. When I saw Jim, I ran to fetch Abraham and Ben with their guns. Ben had the idea to imitate Flint, to give us time to get ahead of you and hide in the bushes."

We made our way off the hill and down to the swamps, where we found the ship's two landing boats. After holing one of the boats to prevent the pirates from following us, we set off on the long row to where I'd hidden the *Hispaniola*. I was relieved to see her drifting free of the sand in the shallows. A high tide and strong winds must have lifted her off the beach. We tied her safe to the shore and left Abraham aboard to guard her decks before rowing around to Rum Cove, the closest beach to Ben Gunn's cave. The squire and doctor greeted me as old friends, with no mention of my having deserted them at the fort.

Inside the large, airy cavern where Ben Gunn lived, I saw a great pile of gold bars, coins, gemstones and other treasures. The thought of all the blood and suffering that this booty had caused my friends, and so many others, made me shudder. I was glad to turn my back on it and sit down for a hearty dinner of goat meat and fine red wine. Silver cooked and served as he had on the voyage, the same polite and dutiful seaman he'd been before the mutiny.

I spent the next three days filling sacks with

gold, while Abraham and the doctor slowly ferried them out to the ship. On the evening before our departure, we left a stash of food, tools and musket powder for the surviving pirates on the island. We'd seen no sign of them since the battle by the pit, but as we sailed away from the island they ran down to the beach and screamed for mercy, pleading with us to take them along and not maroon them. The captain refused. He would not risk another mutiny.

"They'll only hang if we take them home," he told me.

Ten days of storms and hard sailing found us at a port in Spanish America. The captain hoped to take on fresh sailors here to help us on our long voyage home. At dawn the next day, Ben Gunn woke us all and confessed that he'd helped Silver to escape in a little boat during the night.

"I've saved your lives," he cried. "It wasn't safe to have him onboard. None of us would have lived to see England."

That old seadog, one-legged man hadn't gone

empty-handed. He'd snatched a bag of gold to help him on his desperate wanderings. I think we were all pleased to be free of him so cheaply.

The *Hispaniola* reached Bristol safely, with just five survivors from her original crew. We all received a good share of the treasure. Smollett recovered his health and retired from the sea, while Abraham studied to become a mate and bought shares in a merchant ship. Ben Gunn had a thousand pounds, and squandered it in twenty days. The squire gave him a job on his country estate and you can hear the old pirate singing in church every Sunday.

I never heard of Long John again. I hoped he was living in comfort with his wife and parrot somewhere and I wished him no harm; after all, his chances for happiness in the next world are so small.

Some scattered bits of treasure must still be hidden on the island, but wild horses could never drag me back to that place of horrors. In my nightmares, I can hear the surf booming around the island's coast and the voice of Captain Flint ringing like a scream:

"Pieces of eight! Pieces of eight!"

USBORNE QUICKLINKS

For links to websites where you can find out more about Robert Louis Stevenson and his stories, go to the Usborne Quicklinks website at **www.usborne.com/quicklinks** and enter the keywords 'treasure island'. Please follow the online safety guidelines at Usborne Quicklinks.

The websites recommended at Usborne Quicklinks are regularly reviewed, but Usborne Publishing is not responsible and does not accept liability for the availability or content of any website other than its own, or for any exposure to harmful, offensive or inaccurate material which may appear on the Web.